# MOTHER, MC
# I WANT ANO

## by Maria Polushkin
## illustrated by Diane Dawson

**SCHOLASTIC BOOK SERVICES**
NEW YORK · TORONTO · LONDON · AUCKLAND · SYDNEY · TOKYO

ISBN: 0-590-30375-9

12  11  10  9  8  7  6  5  4  3  2                    9/7  0  1  2  3  4/8

Printed in the U.S.A.                                                     07

To Robin

It was bedtime in the mouse house.
Mrs. Mouse took baby mouse to his room.

She helped him put
on his pajamas

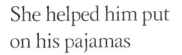

and told him
to brush his teeth.

She tucked him
into his bed

and read him
a bedtime story.

She gave him a bedtime kiss,
and then she said, "Good night."

But as she was leaving,
baby mouse started to cry.
"Why are you crying?" asked Mrs. Mouse.

"I want another, Mother."

"Another mother!" cried
Mrs. Mouse. "Where will I find
another mother for my baby?"

Mrs. Mouse ran to get Mrs. Duck.
"Please, Mrs. Duck, come to our house and help put
baby mouse to bed. Tonight he wants another mother."

Mrs. Duck came and sang a song:

*Quack, quack, mousie,*
*Don't you fret.*
*I'll bring you worms*
*Both fat and wet.*

But baby mouse said,
"Mother, Mother, I want another."

Mrs. Duck went to get Mrs. Frog.

Mrs. Frog came and sang:

*Croak, croak, mousie,*
*Close your eyes.*
*I will bring you*
*Big fat flies.*

But baby mouse said,
"Mother, Mother, I want another."

Mrs. Frog went to get Mrs. Pig.

Mrs. Pig came and sang a song:

*Oink, oink, mousie,*
*Go to sleep.*
*I'll bring some carrots*
*For you to keep.*

But baby mouse said,
"Mother, Mother, I want another."

Mrs. Pig went to get Mrs. Donkey.

Mrs. Donkey came and sang a song:

*Hee-haw, mousie,*
*Hush-a-bye.*
*I'll sing for you*
*A lullaby.*

But baby mouse
had had enough.

"NO MORE MOTHERS!"
he shouted.

"I want another
KISS."

Mrs. Duck
kissed baby mouse.

Mrs. Frog kissed
baby mouse.

Mrs. Pig kissed
baby mouse.

And Mrs. Donkey
kissed baby mouse.

Then Mrs. Mouse gave baby mouse a drink
of water. She tucked in his blanket.

And she gave
him a kiss.

Baby mouse smiled.
"May I have another, Mother?"

"Of course," said Mrs. Mouse, and she
leaned over and gave him *another* kiss.